Pinky Promise

Breaking the code of silence!

By: Alicia J. Turner

Illustrated by: Justin Richburg

The characters and events in this book are fictitious.
Any similarity to real persons, living or dead,
is coincidental and not intended by the author.

Library of Congress Catalog-in-Publication Data has been applied for:
ISBN - 13: 978-0-692-92277-4
ISBN - 10: 0-692-92277-6

Other books by Alicia J. Turner

Who is Ugly?
Ugly never seemed to fit in.
Ugly felt she was ugly, and
Because she believe it,
It was true.

One kind word changed everything, and
Ugly realized she was pretty all along.

**By reading this story,
children will learn the traits of low and high self-esteem,
name calling, and how it relates to bullying.**

Available in English, French, Spanish

The mind of a child is fragile,
their emotions touch their heart,
and words can shape their future.

To learn more about Hey Ugly
visit www.aliciaturner.com

What is a Pinky Promise?

A promise between a child and a responsible adult.

The child promises to tell the responsible adult
anything that makes them uncomfortable,

and the responsible adult promises to
listen, believe, and keep the child safe.

Dear Responsible Adult,

Pinky Promise is about one of the most sensitive topics, one that often goes without thorough discussion, *child sexual abuse.*

This book was written to assist you in starting the conversation with your child in a way that encourages his or her comfort with disclosing secrets. It also served as a fun way to establish a stronger bond between you and your child, characterized by love and trust.

Pinky Promise provides a narrative and illustrations of realistic scenarios, and demonstrates how some unfortunate behaviors, which children and adults are often oblivious, can serve as warning signals of abuse.

This book is not a fairytale, rather it is an educational tool with the primary focus of forging an agreement between child and a responsible adult that will reassure the promise of your protection and safeguard your child from those who wish them harm.

You most likely have already established a strong bond with your child, but do they believe that you can single-handedly protect them? Do they trust in your ability to defend them against anyone or anything, no matter how big or strong, male or female?

Alicia J. Turner

The Interlock

To begin our promise
let's seal the deal with an interlock.

The interlock symbolizes the gesture of commitment,
represented by interlocking your pinky fingers
with someone to seal a promise.

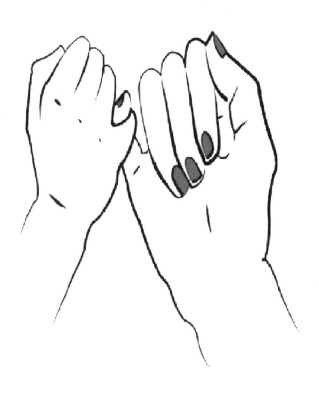

The Promise

Let's make each other this pact,
That we have each other's back.

We don't keep any SECRETS,
And I promise to be there when you need me.

No matter the reason, big or small,
I promise to listen to you whenever you call.

Right or wrong, scared or brave,
I promise to believe you so don't ever be afraid.

We can talk about anything, starting from head to toe,
I promise I can protect you because I am a superhero.

Now our fingers meet arm to arm,
we make this promise to each other
that no one can break this bond.

If a stranger stops
you to say hello,
you can tell me.

If someone calls you
their special friend,
you can tell me.

If your parent's friend
asks to be your friend,
you can tell me.

If someone asks you
to do something you do not like,
you can tell me.

SHHHHHHH.....

If someone talks to you
but never talks to me,
you can tell me.

If someone makes you feel
uncomfortable,
you can tell me.

If someone touches you
and you do not like how it feels,
you can tell me.

If someone asks you
to keep a bad secret,
you can tell me.

And if someone tells you
not to tell me,
Remember our pact,

You promise to tell!

DON'T TELL NOBODY OK...
OK...
WHAT'S WRONG BABY? YOU'VE BEEN QUIET SINCE I GOT YOU FROM YOUR COUSIN'S HOUSE?
NOTHING'S WRONG MOMMY.

Now you make the promise!

Join the conversation and tag your
"Pinky Promise" photos:

@aliciaturnerauthor on Instagram

@_aliciaturner on twitter

@Facebook.com/aliciaturnerauthor

#pinkypromisebook

#imadethepromise

#breakingthecodeofsilence

Visit: www.aliciajturner.com

Pinky Promise

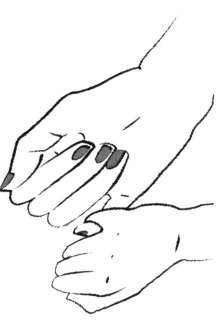

This promise was make on this _____ day of _____, Year _____.

I promise to tell you anything that makes me uncomfortable (Child/ Children).

_____

I promise to LISTEN, BELIEVE, AND PROTECT YOU (Responsible Adult)

_____

BREAKING THE CODE OF SILENCE ONE PROMISE AT A TIME!

SECRET

See a stranger, you're told to yell danger,
But monsters come in different flavors.

Friend or neighbor, coach and nanny,
Sometimes they turn out to be your family.

They knock on your door, tear closets down,
They creep in night when no one is around.

They threatened you not to tell,
And put fear in you not to yell.

They command you to keep your mouth shut,
And promise if you do no one will get hurt.

They hold you to make this awful agreement,
And turn around and call it a **secret**.

You begin to believe that no one understands,
Because they've convinced you that no one cares.

You mind your own business and keep your eyes shut,
But what if you tell, would that monster get locked up?

RESOURCES:

Childhelp — PREVENTION and TREATMENT of CHILD ABUSE.
National Child Abuse Hotline
24 hours a day, 7 days a week.
1-800-4-A-child
1-800-422-4453

Rape, Abuse, & Incest National Network (RAINN)
RAINN is the nation's largest anti-sexual violence organization.
National Sexual Assault Hotline
1-800-656-HOPE
1-800-656-4673

CPSIA information can be obtained
at www.ICGtesting.com
Printed in the USA
BVOW05s0615121117
500201BV00001B/1/P